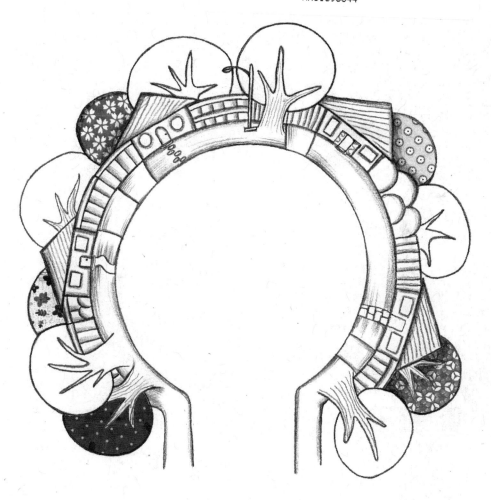

Published by Tradewind Books in Canada in 2012
Text copyright © 2012 Alison Acheson
Illustrations copyright © 2012 Elisa Gutiérrez
Published in the US and the UK in 2013

LIBRARY AND ARCHIVES CANADA
CATALOGUING IN PUBLICATION

Acheson, Alison, 1964-
   The cul-de-sac kids / Alison Acheson ; Elisa Gutiérrez, illustrator.

ISBN 978-1-896580-99-9

   I. Gutiérrez, Elisa, 1972- II. Title.

PS8551.C32C84 2012   jC813'.54   C2012-900648-3

Cataloguing and publication data available from the British Library

Book design by Elisa Gutiérrez
This book is set in Stone Informal.

10 9 8 7 6 5 4 3 2 1

Printed in Canada in March 2012 by Sunrise Printing Chilliwack, BC on FSC ® certified paper using vegetable-based inks.

The publisher thanks the Government of Canada and Canadian Heritage for their financial support through the Canada Council for the Arts, the Canada Book Fund and Livres Canada Books. The publisher also thanks the Government of the Province of British Columbia for the financial support it has given through the Book Publishing Tax Credit program and the British Columbia Arts Council.

Canada Council for the Arts   Conseil des Arts du Canada

BRITISH COLUMBIA ARTS COUNCIL

ALISON ACHESON

The
CUL-DE-SAC

KIDS

illustrations by Elisa Gutiérrez

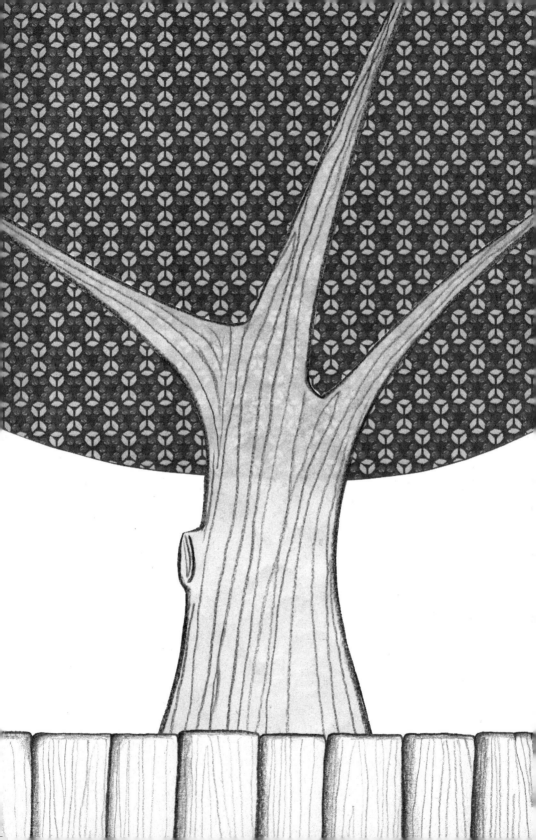

This one is for Emmett—AA

For Daniel, Julia and J.P.—EG

MOVING TRUCK # 1

Kezie and Jed and Patrick watched the moving truck drive away.

Noli was gone.

"I wonder who's moving in," said Kezie.

Jed bumped his hockey stick on the ground impatiently. "Better be someone who plays hockey," he said.

"And bocce!" said Patrick.

Noli's yard was perfect for bocce, and it was Patrick's favourite game.

Jed blasted the ball into the net. "Noli was the best goalie. How are we going to play without her? And now we only have one net."

Kezie didn't answer. She'd spotted something in the hedge. "Look at this!" She held up a dirty pink knitted hat.

"Noli lost that last spring," Patrick said. He reached for the hat, but Kezie held it tight.

Patrick's mouth twisted into a funny shape.

"Are you going to cry?" Kezie asked.

"Maybe later," Patrick said. "Can I have that please?"

"No, I'm going to put it here," said Kezie. She put the pink hat on top of the net. "Where we can share it."

"Come on!" said Jed. "Let's play, already!"

Patrick pulled on the goalie pads and mask. He grabbed Noli's old goalie stick and crouched in the net.

Jed did some stick-handling with the ball—back and forth, back and forth. Then he took a shot and the ball bounced off Patrick's pad . . . right over . . . and in!

Patrick stared at the ball.

Then Kezie shot and hit the goal post.

The hat fell off. Patrick put it back.

Then Jed shot, and Patrick fell over to make the save.

Kezie rescued the hat that time.

"She could have just stayed," grumbled Jed. "Noli could have told her mum she didn't want to move."

"Noli said she had the best mum in the world," Patrick reminded them. Kezie remembered the arguments.

Noli always said she had the mum with the biggest ears, who listened the most.

"But my dad makes the best hot chocolate," said Patrick. Which was true. His dad did. With marshmallows.

Jed went in behind the net to get the ball and bring it around. "What about cookies?" he asked. "Who's going to tell the new kid they live in the Cookie House? What are we going to do about that?"

"Nothing," said Patrick. "We don't know who's moving in. We don't know if they play hockey. Or bocce. Or make cookies. We just know that Noli's gone."

"Are you going to cry?" asked Kezie.

"Yep," said Patrick.

"Is it later now?" asked Kezie.

"Yep," said Patrick, and he sat down in the net. Jed shot the ball in from the side. Noli's hat fell and landed on Patrick's head.

"C'mon," said Jed. "We've got to play two-on-one. Until the new neighbour comes along."

13

At the end of the week, another moving truck arrived. This truck wasn't as big as Noli's. This truck didn't have many things in it.

"I don't see any bikes," said Kezie.

"Or hockey sticks," said Jed.

Patrick shook his head.

The movers went past carrying a green couch. Its colour made Patrick think of spinach.

Kezie wondered why someone would have only two chairs with their kitchen table. She handed Patrick the goalie mask. They began to play

15

two-on-one, which wasn't much fun because Jed kept taking the ball away and running around the cul-de-sac. But he stopped when a car drove into Noli's driveway.

"There he is," said Jed, "or she . . . our new goalie . . . or player. Or maybe even two . . . or three."

They watched as a lone man climbed out of the car. He was wearing a very neat suit and round eyeglasses. He looked at the hockey net and frowned. Patrick put up his hand to wave, but when the man squinted at him, Patrick dropped his hand.

The man went into Noli's old house.

"He didn't even say hi," said Kezie.

"There's no way he plays hockey," said Jed. "Did you see how he looked at the net?"

"I know what you mean," said Kezie. She sounded disappointed.

Patrick walked up to the car. He peered
in and shook his head. He couldn't believe
it. "There aren't any kids!"

..

"The man's name is Mr. McNeil," Kezie told the others the next morning. "My mum says it's just him."

"No kids?" asked Patrick.

"No kids. And Mum said he's going to rattle around in that big house."

"Huh?" said Jed.

"That's what *I* said, and my mum told me to say 'Pardon?' like she always does."

"Pardon?" said Jed, because he knew that if he didn't, Kezie wouldn't tell him the rest of the story.

"My mum said that means he's going to be lonely."

"He's going to be lonely because he's so grumpy!" said Patrick. "He has a huge frown."

Just then Mr. McNeil drove up again. And just like the day before, he got out of his car, looked over his glasses and frowned.

"He didn't frown at *us*!" Jed pointed out. "He frowned at the hockey net."

"And he didn't rattle," said Patrick.

"That just happens when he's all by himself in the house," said Kezie.

"Maybe he should just stay outside," said Jed.

· ·

The day after that, when Mr. McNeil drove up, Jed held out his old hockey stick.

"I bet you don't play hockey," said Jed.

Mr. McNeil looked startled. "You're right. I used to play baseball." He didn't take the hockey stick.

Patrick cleared his throat as if he was going to say something. Something important.

"Yes?" said Mr. McNeil.

"Kids!" Patrick finally said. "Do you have any kids? Even just one?"

"No," said Mr. McNeil.

"That's too bad," said Patrick.

"We need a hockey player," said Jed.

"Noli was our goalie," said Kezie.

Mr. McNeil scratched his head. "I will be getting two kids soon—Henry and Daisy. Henry's about your age, Daisy is younger." Then he hurried into the house.

Jed felt as if a cloud had dropped a load of hot dogs on his head. "Huh?" he said. "How do you get two kids soon? How does that work?"

Patrick and Kezie stared after Mr. McNeil and shook their heads. They didn't know.

"Do you hear any rattling?" whispered Jed.

"None," said Patrick.

Kezie whispered too. "I hear a bit."

Patrick tried hard, but couldn't hear anything. "Maybe this will all work out," he said. But Jed and Kezie shook their heads.

○ THE FENCE ○

There had always been four boards missing in the fence between Noli's old house and Kezie's. It had been a perfect door. But on Saturday they discovered that the hole was almost gone. Two yellow boards

were there. As they watched, Mr. McNeil pushed a third board into place and began to hammer. He gave a loud yell and stopped hammering for a minute. But only for a minute. Up went a fourth board.

The fence no longer had a door. It was just a fence.

Kezie looked at the bright boards. Now she wanted to sit in the hockey net and cry. "Don't people have to ask other people if they want to fix things?" she asked. "Isn't there a law about that?"

"Mr. McNeil doesn't even know kids need holes in fences," said Jed in a fierce voice.

They heard a screen door bounce open—and voices. Voices of kids.

"Do you hear that?" asked Kezie.

Patrick's eyes were big.

"That must be them," said Jed. "He wasn't making it up. Mr. McNeil got his kids."

"He's going to be our dad," said a voice.

Kezie, Patrick and Jed looked up and saw a girl and a boy climbing into a tree next to the fence.

"And he's going to be the best!" the girl added as she settled onto a branch.

"He is?" asked Patrick.

The boy nodded, peering down from the branches. "He's going to marry our mum. Next month. That's when we're moving in. He's going to be our new dad." He was wearing a bright red hockey jersey.

Jed's face brightened. "You play hockey!" he said. Then his face looked less bright. "But Mr. McNeil . . ." he started to say.

Kezie reached out and grabbed his elbow. She gave it a shake. "What?" he turned to ask.

Just then a woman's voice called the girl and the boy to come for lunch.

"Why'd you do that?" Jed asked when they left.

"Because you were going to say something, weren't you?"

"Like what?"

"I don't know," said Kezie. "But I had a feeling it wasn't going to be nice."

"Somebody should tell them, don't you think? They need to know."

"Know what?"

"Know that Mr. McNeil is grumpy and doesn't play hockey!"

Kezie didn't argue. "You're right," she said. "He doesn't even have enough chairs!"

"And he ruined the fence," Patrick pointed out.

Jed tried to spy through the narrow space between the fence boards, but it was no use.

"A month isn't very long, is it?" said Kezie.

"It took my dad two summers to learn how to roast marshmallows," Patrick said.

"My dad will never learn that," said Jed. "He likes to light them on fire."

Next day, there was a surprise. Noli's net was standing in its usual spot in the cul-de-sac.

"I wonder where it came from," Kezie said.

"Maybe Noli's back!" shouted Patrick.

Just then Mr. McNeil came out. "I found it in the workshop," he said. "There was a note on it."

For my friends, Kezie and Jed and Patrick.
I hope the people who move into my
house are hockey players!
I will visit next summer.
Noli

Mr. McNeil scratched his head. "The boy who's going to be my son—Henry—loves ice hockey. He's trying out for a special team."

"We know. We met him," said Patrick. "You should play too."

"If you can," added Jed.

"Jed!" said Kezie.

"I don't play hockey," Mr. McNeil said. "I'm too old and rusty."

"Is that why you rattle?" asked Jed.

"Who said anything about rattling?" said Mr. McNeil.

"Noli always played goal," Kezie said.

"And your house is the Cookie House," said Jed. "Kezie's is the Peanut Butter Sandwich House. Patrick's is Hot Chocolate. My house is the Random Snack House."

"I live in the Cookie House?"

"That means you only have to worry about one thing," said Jed. "My house does

Snacks. Your house does Cookies. Chocolate chip cookies."

"But houses don't bake cookies," said Mr. McNeil. "People do." He looked worried.

"For now, just play goal," said Jed.

After a long minute, it seemed that Mr. McNeil decided that arguing with Jed wasn't worth it, and he moved into the net.

"Noli always wore her pink hat when she played goal," said Jed. "She said it was her lucky hat."

"She left it behind," said Kezie. "You could use it."

Patrick crumpled a bit when she said that.

"That is," said Kezie, "if it's okay with Patrick."

Patrick thought for a minute. "It's okay with me."

Kezie handed the hat to Mr. McNeil. Jed handed him the stick.

The game was on.

Every single shot got by Mr. McNeil.

"You're not supposed to move out of the way when the puck's coming!" said Jed.

"It's a ball," said Mr. McNeil.

"It's a puck!" said Kezie, Patrick and Jed.

"I don't want to get hit," said Mr. McNeil.

Jed shook his head. "But it's only a ball. It won't hurt you."

"Use your glove more," suggested Patrick.

"Flash the leather," corrected Jed.

"Flash the leather," repeated Patrick and Mr. McNeil.

"Just use your glove," said Kezie.

"When you see the puck coming," said Jed, "get in the way, quick!"

"I'll try that," said Mr. McNeil. But a few more shots went right into the net.

"This isn't going to work," he said.

He went into his house and rattled around.

"I think we're in trouble," said Kezie.

"What sort of trouble?" asked Patrick.

"Do you think Mr. McNeil is ready to be a dad?" Kezie asked.

"No!" said Jed.

Kezie was worried. She was thinking of the girl up in the tree, looking over the fence and saying, "He's going to be the best."

"Maybe we can do something," she said.

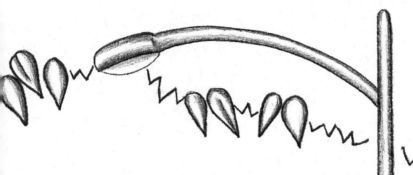

"Like what?" asked Jed.

"Like maybe we could teach him a few things. A bit of hockey. Maybe how to make cookies."

"Maybe he'll be okay with the roasting marshmallow thing," said Patrick.

Jed looked doubtful.

"It's worth a try. If we can't fix him, there'll never be another kid living in that house," said Kezie.

On Saturday a big pile of dirt was delivered to the end of Mr. McNeil's driveway. Patrick wondered if they could play in it.

Kezie said, "If we're going to teach Mr. McNeil, maybe we should make a report card for him. We could start by seeing what he does with that dirt. It'll be like a test."

Jed said, "I bet he'll just ask us to put it in all those planter things."

But Mr. McNeil didn't say anything about planters or playing. He came out with his shirt sleeves rolled up, and he began to shovel the dirt here and there in the yard. "I need to fill in these holes," he said. "There are so many."

No one wanted to tell him about the time they tried to find buried treasure in the yard. It was so hard to follow the directions on the map drawn by Noli's dad.

"He's ruining it for bocce," said Patrick sadly. "A good bocce yard needs lots of holes."

"No it doesn't," said Kezie. Her bocce balls always got stuck in the holes.

"The yard has to be ready for the wedding day," Mr. McNeil said. "It's going to be a Big Day." He unrolled something that looked like grass carpet. He called it "turf." As they watched, he cut pieces from it and began to cover the holes with them. It was strange.

"I don't think he knows what he's doing," said Jed.

Patrick spoke up. "My dad says that Mr. McNeil knows exactly what he's doing. He says he's a very spear-the-ants gardener."

"I think you mean *experienced* gardener," Kezie said.

"Humph," said Jed. "Mr. McNeil might know about ants, but he doesn't know about yards!"

"Maybe we could give him an A for ants!" said Patrick.

"We haven't really seen him with ants," Kezie was quick to point out.

Then Mr. McNeil went into his backyard to work, and the three kids went to Kezie's.

They stared at the new yellow fence boards, until at last Mr. McNeil came out through the side gate. "That's better!" he said. "Good as a golf green!"

"That's better," said Jed, "if you like golf." He did an ahem thing, and cleared his throat, as if he had an announcement to make. "We think that maybe we could teach you a few things—about how to be a dad."

Mr. McNeil looked surprised. "You think I need that?"

"We do . . ." Jed started to say.

Kezie spoke up quickly. "Maybe just some more hockey practice for now," she said.

Patrick handed the goalie stick to Mr. McNeil. Jed ran around stick-handling and returned to drill in one of his faster-than-lightning shots.

The ball went right by Mr. McNeil.

"Bocce's a lot like golf," Jed said, as he watched Mr. McNeil recover from the shot.

"It is?" asked Mr. McNeil.

"Sure. You just follow the little white ball around."

Jed took another shot. It went in too.

"Hmmm," said Mr. McNeil. "I never thought of it like that."

"But you've ruined it now," said Jed.

"Ruined?" asked Mr. McNeil.

"Noli had the all-time best bocce yard," said Patrick.

Mr. McNeil looked puzzled.

"It was full of holes," explained Kezie.

"Oh," said Mr. McNeil. "Holes."

"A good bocce yard should look like a hundred gophers live in it. Just like how Noli's yard looked before you ruined it," said Jed. Then he took another shot. It went in. "That's a hat trick," he added.

"A hat trick?" said Mr. McNeil. "How's this?" He snatched up the pink hat and pulled it on almost over his eyes.

But Jed shook his head. "That won't help," he said sadly. "A hat trick is when I get three goals, just like that, one after the other, while you stand there."

Mr. McNeil rolled up his sleeve, looked at his watch and said, "Henry and Daisy are coming over." He seemed glad to change the subject. "Do you have an extra hockey stick?"

"Sure," said Patrick. "But we'll need two, won't we?"

"Oh," said Mr. McNeil, "I really don't want to play."

"Yes you do," said Jed. "You need to keep practising!"

A car pulled up and out came Henry and Daisy.

Patrick gave them each a stick, and Jed said, "Mr. McNeil's going to play in goal. Patrick and Daisy, you be on his team. I'll be the other goalie. Kezie and Henry can be on my team."

Jed threw down the puck for the faceoff and raced to his net.

Daisy took a shot that went wide, and Mr. McNeil missed it. The puck flew into Jed's yard. They watched Mr. McNeil run after it.

Patrick asked, "Do you think Mr. McNeil knows how much he has to learn?"

"I don't think he has a clue," said Jed.

"Learn about what?" asked Henry.

Jed pretended he didn't see Kezie's warning look. He said, "About being a dad."

"Right," said Henry. "I don't think he has even half a clue."

"I think he has a half!" said Daisy. "A big half." But she did look worried.

A big truck pulled into the cul-de-sac. The words FANNY'S FURNITURE were painted on the side. Two delivery men carted a wooden table and four chairs through Mr. McNeil's front door.

Kezie pulled out her report card notepad. Chairs, she wrote. And next to it, a B.

"Why a B?" asked Patrick. "Why not an A?"

"Because two chairs plus four equals only six. If all three of us visit, there won't be enough."

"You should write a C then!" said Jed.

Kezie crossed out the B, and wrote C.

Jed looked over her shoulder at the notebook. "You gave him an F for being goalie," he said. "That's absolutely right!"

A car drove up. Daisy and Henry hopped out. So did a woman with bright red hair.

"Their mum!" said Kezie.

Henry had hockey trophies and rolled-up posters in his arms. Daisy had a trumpet and stuffed rabbit.

The mum smiled. "You're the kids Daisy and Henry were telling me about," she said. "Fred says you're teaching him to play hockey."

Fred must be Mr. McNeil.

"That's not all we're teaching," said Jed.

The red-haired woman looked puzzled.

"We're fixing him," explained Jed.

"We should be finished with him in time for the wedding," added Patrick.

"Fixing him? Finished with him?" The red-haired woman shook her head and headed for the door.

"We'll let you know when he's ready," Patrick said.

"I'm sure everything will be just fine," she called out over her shoulder.

The boy, Henry, watched her go. "That's what my mum always says: 'Everything will be just fine.' Sometimes she's right," he added.

"She's always right," said his sister.

"How's the teaching going?" Henry asked Patrick.

"All right," Patrick started to say, but Jed interrupted him.

"It's not going well," said Jed. "In fact, he has an F in hockey, and a C in . . ."

"What's that?" Daisy asked. "I smell something."

"That's Patrick's socks," said Kezie. Patrick liked to take his shoes off, but leave his

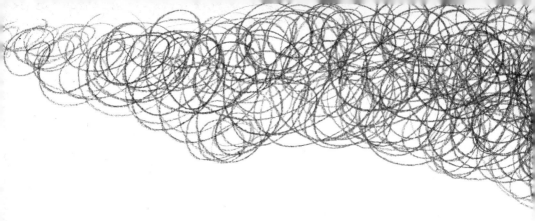

socks on, when he wasn't playing hockey. Even outside.

"No," said Patrick, "it's not my socks."

"It's FIRE!" yelled Jed. He jumped up and waved his arms toward the kitchen window of Mr. McNeil's house.

"It's smoke!" said Daisy.

Smoke was pouring out of the window, and they could hear the beep beep of the alarm.

"We have to get your mum and Mr. McNeil out!" Jed said, and ran to the front door.

It opened. "Everything's just fine!" the red-headed woman said. Her hair was standing on end, but she was smiling. "It's Fred," she said. "He's baking cookies!"

Mr. McNeil came to the door with a cookie sheet. His hand was covered with a yellow happy-face oven mitt. "Chocolate chip! Just like you said." He pulled one off—it was stuck to the pan—and blew on it to cool. He took a bite.

"That's a burnt cookie," Jed pointed out.

Mr. McNeil chewed. "It's fine," he said. "Really." Another bite of the black-brown cookie. "It's just like the ones my mum used to make!" He finished it off.

Henry turned to the others. "You'd better keep going with that teaching thing," he whispered. He and Daisy both looked worried. They followed Mr. McNeil into the house.

"So," muttered Jed, "another big F on Mr. McNeil's report card."

"This isn't good," Kezie said. She looked worried too. "He needs real sit-down school.

Dad School. He needs to go every day. Starting tomorrow."

"Let's give him detention!" said Jed.

DAD SCHOOL

Kezie and Jed found two wooden crates and built a desk. Jed drew a sign and Patrick filled in the letters: DAD SCHOOL.

When they knocked on the door, Mr. McNeil answered. He took a look at what they'd made in the cul-de-sac.

"Is that for me?" he asked.

They nodded.

"You really think I need it?"

They nodded.

"I thought my goaltending was getting pretty good."

They shook their heads.

"Shall I bring some cookies for us to share?"

"No!" they all shouted quickly.

"Maybe you like burnt cookies, but we don't," said Jed.

So Mr. McNeil followed them out to the desk and sat down with the paper and pencil that Jed handed him. It was different having three teachers and one student.

"Always remember," began Patrick, "to put lots of butter on popcorn."

"Tons of butter," added Kezie, and she watched to make sure Mr. McNeil was taking notes.

Butter, Mr. McNeil wrote.

"You have to make sure your kids wear bike helmets," went on Patrick.

"And make sure Henry's wearing his undershirt if he has a cold and his grandma's coming over," said Jed.

"What?" said Kezie, turning to him.

"My grandma says I get sick because I don't wear an undershirt."

Helmets. Undershirt, Mr. McNeil wrote.

"I don't know about that," said Kezie, "but whatever you do, don't wash Daisy's stuffed rabbit."

Mr. McNeil began to look nervous then, as if he really needed to go somewhere.

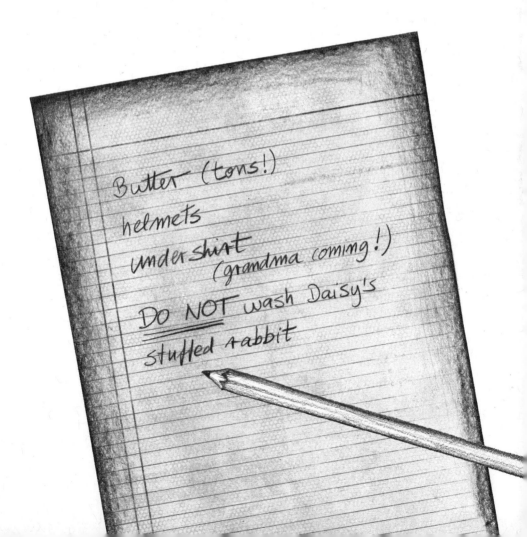

Butter (tons!)
helmets
undershirt
(grandma coming!)
DO NOT wash Daisy's
stuffed rabbit

"Mostly, though," said Jed, "we need to talk about your yard and bocce and the fence."

Mr. McNeil stood up to go, but Jed gently pushed him back into the chair. "Maybe," he said, "you should build a tree house."

"Or something," added Kezie.

Yard. Fence. Build something, wrote Mr. McNeil. Then he looked at his paper and shook his head as if he wasn't sure what was going on.

"Anything else?" he asked.

"Yes," said Kezie. "You've got to know what to say when they run away!"

Mr. McNeil looked shocked. "Run away?" he asked.

"All kids run away," said Kezie.

"I've never run away," said Jed.

"Except Jed," Kezie said.

"Why would you run away?" asked Mr. McNeil.

"Because Mum gave me Grandma's little suitcase and it was bright green and I had to use it," said Kezie.

"I ran away because I was mad at my sister," said Patrick.

"About what?" asked Mr. McNeil.

"About something important."

"So what am I supposed to do?"

"Remind them that Riley has a birthday party tomorrow," said Patrick.

Mr. McNeil was looking very confused. "Who's Riley?"

"Doesn't matter. There's always some kid with a birthday tomorrow. And you might miss it if you run away."

"Or there might be ice cream melting on the counter," said Jed.

"Am I going to be tested on all this?" asked Mr. McNeil.

"We'll tell you everything you need to pass," said Kezie. "Don't worry about it."

Jed scowled. "Worry about it!" he said.

"I think you need just one more test," Patrick spoke up quickly. "Soon. Build something. Just do everything right, and you'll be fine."

BUILD SOME- THING

"I'm not good at building," Mr. McNeil said the next day. He showed Kezie, Patrick and Jed a dark blue thumbnail. "I hit it with the hammer when I fixed the fence," he said. "I thought I'd set up a tent instead."

There was a big open box on the ground. Daisy was pulling bright green fabric out of it, and Henry had made a pile of long metal poles.

"Noli's dad could set up a tent in two minutes," said Jed, almost sounding helpful.

Mr. McNeil spread out the fabric. "Is this the front?" he asked.

Jed shook his head, but he didn't say anything more about the tent. Instead he said,

"I'm going home for a Random Snack."
And he hurried away as if he couldn't take
any more tent-talk.

He came back moments later with a bag
of pretzels. "Mum tried to give me carrot
sticks, but I said no."

"I like carrot sticks," said Mr. McNeil.

"I don't live in the Carrot Stick House,"
Jed reminded Mr. McNeil.

Patrick waved his hand at the tent,
which was still lying on the ground. "The
front of the tent should have a door in it,"
he said. "That's a window."

"You could climb through the window if
you had to, though, right?" Mr. McNeil
sounded hopeful. He looked at the picture
on the box.

Henry found the directions. "I think these
go here," he said, and pushed together some
of the poles. Mr. McNeil put them into the

edges of the fabric just like in the pictures. It
began to look something like a tent.

Then Daisy found some leftover bits.

"I think all the parts are supposed to have

a place," said Jed. "Like puzzle pieces."

They looked through the directions and found places for most of the extra parts.

At the end of the afternoon, the tent was

up—sort of. The door zipper was caught, but at least it was half open.

"You're not finished, are you?" asked Kezie. She didn't want to have to fill in the report card yet. Not until every one of the pieces had a place.

"I think we need a break," said Mr. McNeil.

"I think so too!" said Daisy. "You've been working really hard."

"Would all of you like to stay for pizza?" Mr. McNeil asked.

"Pizza," Patrick whispered to Kezie. "We might just have to give him an A for this!"

"Yes," said Kezie. "We can add it as another assignment." She wrote Pizza in the notebook.

The pizza arrived and Mr. McNeil opened the box.

"There's too much stuff on that pizza!" Patrick blurted. He turned a bit red. He didn't mean to be rude.

"Yeah . . . what's all that green and purple and yellow stuff?" asked Jed. "There shouldn't be any green on a pizza!"

Kezie looked. "Peppers and onion and more peppers."

Jed poked at something. "Meat," he said. "Meatballs. Little ones. That's okay." He spoke into Patrick's ear. "We should have told Mr. McNeil about pizza a long time ago—like, first thing."

"This pizza has so much more on it than a plain old pepperoni one," said Mr. McNeil as he handed a piece to Daisy. "And it's even the same price!"

"This will be good," said Daisy. "It really will."

Mr. McNeil looked grateful. But Kezie noticed that Daisy picked off all the peppers when she thought nobody was looking.

Next to Pizza, Kezie wrote an F.

"I know!" said Daisy. "Let's eat the pizza out in the tent!"

••

It was supposed to be a five-person tent. Jed and Henry and Kezie sat together at one end while Patrick and Daisy crouched under the falling-down roof.

"So? It's looking good, isn't it?" said Mr. McNeil. He poked his head through the window, and it was as if a storm blew through. The tent poles shook, the flysheet made a noise like crashing waves, and the whole thing fell to the ground.

Patrick never did find his pizza in all the green fabric. And Kezie thought Mr. McNeil looked as if he wanted to run away.

Next to Tent-building, she would have to write another F.

Time to go home. Kezie went next door to her house, and Jed and Patrick crossed the cul-de-sac to their homes.

"This isn't good," said Patrick gloomily.

"Not good at all," said Jed.

Tomorrow was Mr. McNeil's wedding, and he had only one day left to pass Dad School. But Kezie couldn't find her notebook with his grades in it. "Maybe I left it at Mr. McNeil's," she said to Jed and Patrick.

"That wouldn't be good," said Patrick.

Kezie and Jed and Patrick went to Mr. McNeil's house, but he was nowhere to be seen.

"We promised to help decorate," Patrick told Daisy and Henry's mum when she answered the door. "Where's Mr. McNeil?" Kezie asked.

"He was running out the door when we arrived," said the red-headed woman. "He said he had things to do. I'm sure he'll be back any minute."

Kezie took a quick peek in the kitchen, but didn't see the notebook. She wondered if Mr. McNeil had it with him, wherever he was.

Patrick whispered, "You don't think Mr. McNeil found the report card and ran away, do you?"

Jed said, "I'd run away if it was my report card!"

Daisy and Henry's mum picked up a ladder. "Let's get started with the decorating," she said. "We have only one more day. We need ivy cut off the fence and brought in. And I have these little twinkly lights."

She gathered up all the boxes of lights and began to open them. Her red hair was wild and her eyes were shiny. Mr. McNeil's running away didn't seem to bother her. She kept saying, "Everything will be just fine!"

"What was it that Mr. McNeil had to do?" asked Kezie.

"I'm not sure. He just went out with a long list in his hand!"

Kezie wondered if the long list looked anything like a notebook.

They cut the ivy and brought it in. Patrick spilled some water, but Daisy and Henry's mum said not to worry, everything would be fine. They began to hang up the ivy, all around the room. Jed tripped over one of the dangling vines, and a chair crashed, but she still said the same thing.

"It's so pretty!" she told them when they'd finished.

A truck came by to drop off rented chairs. There would be lots of chairs for people to sit on.

"Now they have enough chairs," Patrick pointed out to Kezie. But she couldn't change the report card, because it was still missing.

"Besides," she said, "they're here only for one day."

The kids set up the chairs in rows across the main room, and still Mr. McNeil didn't return.

"Let's decorate the front doorway," said Henry and Daisy's mum, and she opened the front door.

There was Mr. McNeil with a box of doughnuts.

"So he didn't run away!" whispered Kezie.

"I'll bet he did, but changed his mind!" said Jed.

Mr. McNeil gave everyone a doughnut.

He brought around a short stepladder and more fancy lights.

Jed climbed the ladder and hung the lights. Then Daisy wanted to try. So Mr. McNeil moved the ladder to the other side and held it, while Daisy scrambled up. She reached for the hooks on the other side, but they were a bit too high for her and her foot slipped. Mr. McNeil caught Daisy, but not before she knocked her knee on a ladder rung.

"Ow!" she cried.

Mr. McNeil sat on the steps. He gave her a hug and a crinkly tissue from his pocket. He took a look at the knee. They decided it was going to be all right. Maybe a bit red, but all right.

"What grade are you going to give him for that?" Patrick asked Kezie. She forgot that the report card was missing and reached into her pocket.

"If I had it," she whispered to Patrick, "I'd mark it with an A!"

"It'll turn up," he said. "After all, Mr. McNeil did."

They finished the doorway. Patrick made huge bows out of white ribbon. Kezie and Henry blew up golden balloons. Jed finished the lights, and Daisy put a new WELCOME TO OUR HOME mat in front of the door.

When they were done, they all stood back to look at it just as the phone rang.

F for...

"It's for you, Henry," said his mum. She held out the phone.

He took it and went inside.

"I think it's the hockey coach," his mum said. Mr. McNeil crossed his fingers on both hands. Then he crossed his eyes and shut them tight as if he were making a wish.

Everyone pretended to be busy putting away the decorating tools. Really, they were waiting to hear Henry's news about the hockey team.

When he came back, Henry was trying hard not to cry.

"Let's go for a walk," said Mr. McNeil in a low voice. He and Henry walked out of the cul-de-sac and down the street. Mr. McNeil had his big hand on Henry's shoulder, and he tilted his head down to listen.

The other kids gathered close together at the end of the driveway and watched.

"Do you remember what Noli used to say about her mum?" asked Kezie. "How her mum had the biggest ears?"

Patrick nodded. "She said her mum was the best listener ever."

"I think Mr. McNeil's like that," Kezie said.

She waved as Mr. McNeil and Henry turned around and headed back toward them. Henry was laughing at something his almost-dad said to him.

"The thing to remember," said Patrick suddenly, "is that there's always street hockey."

"Oh yeah!" said Kezie. She went to gather the hockey sticks.

Patrick set up the nets.

Henry and Daisy's mum said she'd get some juice and a snack.

"My mum might still have those carrot sticks," said Jed, and he went to find out.

They were ready to play by the time Henry and Mr. McNeil returned. Mr. McNeil reached for the pink hat and grabbed his goalie stick. He gave the hat to Daisy, though, when she said she wanted to be the other goalie. "For Noli luck," he told her.

Jed handed a stick to Henry. Henry looked at it for a minute, grabbed it and then grinned.

After a short version of the national anthem, they dropped the puck. Jed won the faceoff and deked past Kezie. Then Henry stole the puck and took a shot on Mr. McNeil, who for once tried hard to get in the way, but no—in slid the puck!

Mr. McNeil sat in the net, rubbing his knee.

"That was a great goal, Henry!" shouted Patrick. "And you almost got it, Mr. McNeil!" he added.

Daisy said something about getting ice, and ran into the house.

"You know," said Jed, thumping his stick on the ground, "I think you're starting to get the hang of this game."

Mr. McNeil stopped rubbing his knee. "You think?" he asked as he stood.

"We think so too," added Kezie and Patrick.

Mr. McNeil looked quite pleased at that. And hobbled off to sit on the stairs.

Daisy came out the door and handed him a bag of frozen peas. Then she ran over to Kezie and the other kids. She had something in her hand. "Who does this belong to? I just found it," she said.

The notebook.

"That's mine," Kezie said in a whisper. She could see that Daisy had the notebook open to the page with all of Mr. McNeil's grades.

Goalie F
Chairs F
Cookies F
tent
building F

"That looks like a report card," said Henry, looking over his sister's shoulder. "Is that part of your school for our new dad?"

Kezie nodded.

"That can't be right," said Daisy. "There are so many Fs. What are they for?"

"Well . . ." Jed started to say.

"Be quiet, Jed." Kezie stared at the pencil marks. What could all those Fs be for? "We got it all wrong," she said to Daisy, who was looking up at her with such hope. She looked over at Mr. McNeil, who was sitting on the steps with the bag of frozen peas on his knee. He was smiling at Daisy and Henry's mum, and she was laughing.

"I know you were worried," Henry said, "but I think he's going to be a pretty good dad."

"So do I," Kezie said. "And you said he was going to be the best dad ever, didn't you?" she asked Daisy.

"Of course I did," Daisy said.

"Well, then, they're for Fine," said Kezie. "Everything is just Fine!"

Daisy thought about that for a moment. "I knew that," she said, with a wide smile. "That sounds right!"

"Do you think our new dad needs to know that everything's just fine?" Henry asked Daisy.

"Yes—he needs to know too," said Daisy.

"We should give him a diploma," said Jed.

"I have an even better idea!" Patrick spoke up.

. .

Next day, Kezie, Patrick and Jed found Mr. McNeil in his backyard. He was wearing a tuxedo and he was holding up a piece of paper. The kids saw that it was his Dad School notes.

Mr. McNeil was checking off something. He rolled up the paper and tucked it into his pocket, then picked up his hammer and waved it around. "How would you feel about me pulling out these new fence boards?" he asked. "I realized I never asked you if I could fix things."

"We never asked you either," said Jed.

Mr. McNeil looked confused at that, but no more than usual. They each took off a board.

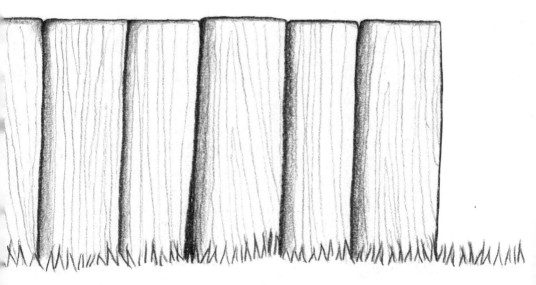

The fence-door was open again.

"We made something for you," said Patrick.

"For me?" asked Mr. McNeil, surprised.

Kezie handed him a square black thing.

Mr. McNeil realized what it was and grinned. He put it on his head. "My graduation cap," he said. "I like the fancy tassel."

"It wasn't Pizza School, or Tent-building School," said Jed. "It was Dad School . . . so you passed."

"Why, thank you!" said Mr. McNeil.

"Hey!" shouted Patrick. "It's snowing!"

"No it's not," said Jed.

"It's confetti!" said Kezie. There was a blizzard of little white bits from the tree, and everyone looked up to see Daisy and Henry sitting on a branch and giggling.

Jed looked closely at a few of the bits. "I know what this is!" he said and threw them up into the air again.

All the little white bits floated down, until Noli's old backyard was filled with paper snow and laughter.

ALISON ACHESON has written many books for children and young people. Her young adult novel *Mud Girl* was a finalist for the Canadian Library Association's Young Adult Book Award. Alison teaches writers of all ages and works as a freelance editor. She lives in Ladner, BC, with her spouse, three sons and an old rescue dog named Rocky. Check out www.alisonacheson.com.

ELISA GUTIÉRREZ is a graphic designer and illustrator. Her book *Picturescape* was short-listed for the Christie Harris Illustrated Children's Literature Prize. Her graphic design has been recognized many times by the Alcuin Society Awards for Excellence in Book Design. She lives and works in Vancouver, BC, with her family.